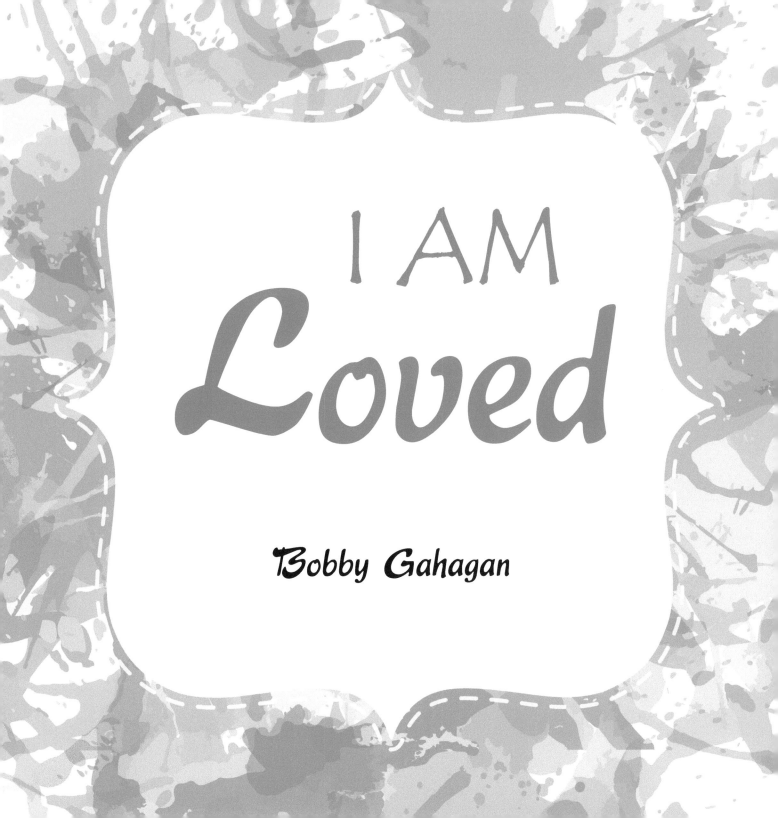

I AM
Loved

Bobby Gahagan

Illustrated by: Jessica Miller
Email: jessmiller1124@gmail.com

Library of Congress Control Number: 2020923723

HARDBACK: 978-1-953791-56-6
PAPERBACK: 978-1-953791-55-9
EBOOK: 978-1-953791-57-3

Ordering Information:

For orders and inquiries, please contact:
1-888-404-1388
www.goldtouchpress.com
book.orders@goldtouchpress.com

Printed in the United States of America

Dedication

To: K.N.Y.
Thank you for your friendship,
support and inspiration.
Without you this book would not be possible.

To: Jessica,
Thank you for lending your talents to this project,
you made it come alive.

Hello, my name is Willow. As you can see from my picture,
I am a very happy little girl!

Do you want to know why I am so happy?
It's because I am loved! How do I know this?
Because everyone says to me, "I love you!"

That may seem a simple enough statement
but not everyone gets to hear it often enough. You see,
I have a wonderful family and group of friends that tells me so,
and shows me all the time just how much they care about me.

Never a day goes by that I don't hear those wonderful and encouraging
words from the people that I am close to. It fills me with warmth and
happiness to know that I am cared about and cared for.

Not everyone out there has the same support that I have and that's alright, because no matter your situation, there are people in your life that love and care for you.

There are many family members and friends that visit often. They all have one thing in common, they all say that they love me! How wonderful a feeling is that? It is of no wonder that I am always so happy looking! How can I not be when so many people show me so much love?

Everyone needs love in their life. No matter if it's from family, friends or care givers. Love is essential to being happy.

Speaking of family; here is mine! Now I don't want to brag, but I do have a very handsome daddy and a very beautiful mommy and my brother is a cutie pie. At least as far as brothers go anyhow. So I know I will be just as cute as cute can be when I grow up!

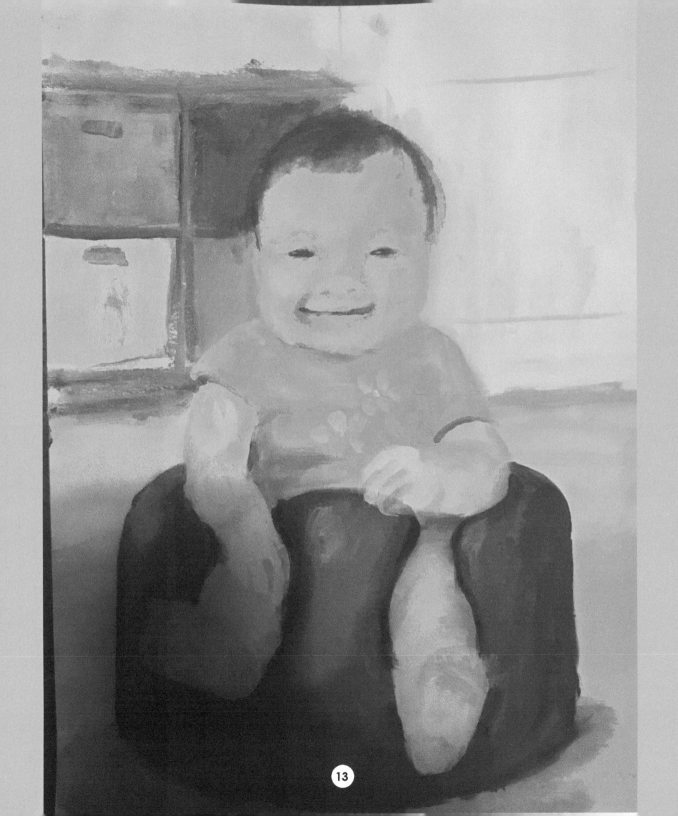

Even now I am slowly changing my looks to become my very own unique person. And that's good, because everyone I see looks different. There is no need to worry over what you look like because people will all be different in some way or another. And that is good because it would be boring if we were all the same!

There are times when people come to visit and they bring gifts. But it can be so confusing what to play with when I have so much to choose from. And you know what my favorite thing to play with is? People! That's right, my family and friends are my favorite. They get down on the floor or pick me up and hold me on the couch and play with me. That's the best!

I get so excited to see them come and visit that I get to smiling and laughing and pumping my arms and legs in the air just to let out all the joy that I'm experiencing. And guess what? They seem to enjoy it too! For then they start to laugh and smile right along with me. We have such wonderful times that I don't want them to end! Then there are the times when they sing to me. It can be a wonderful experience! No matter what the song is or how bad they mess up the words, it is great to hear their voice singing to me. Just to know that it is for me and only me they do it shows how much they care!

Every once and a while I get to go outside. The sights and sounds are so overwhelming! Birds are chirping out their songs and the feel of the wind as it blows over my face and hands actually tickles me. The sun is so warming to me that it makes me feel sleepy sometimes. It also feels like I'm being held by my mom or dad, it is so warm and comfy! I can't wait till I'm old enough to run around like my big brother does out here, it seems like fun! For now though, I have to stay in my little area inside a crib outside. But no matter, soon enough I'll be able to run and jump and play!

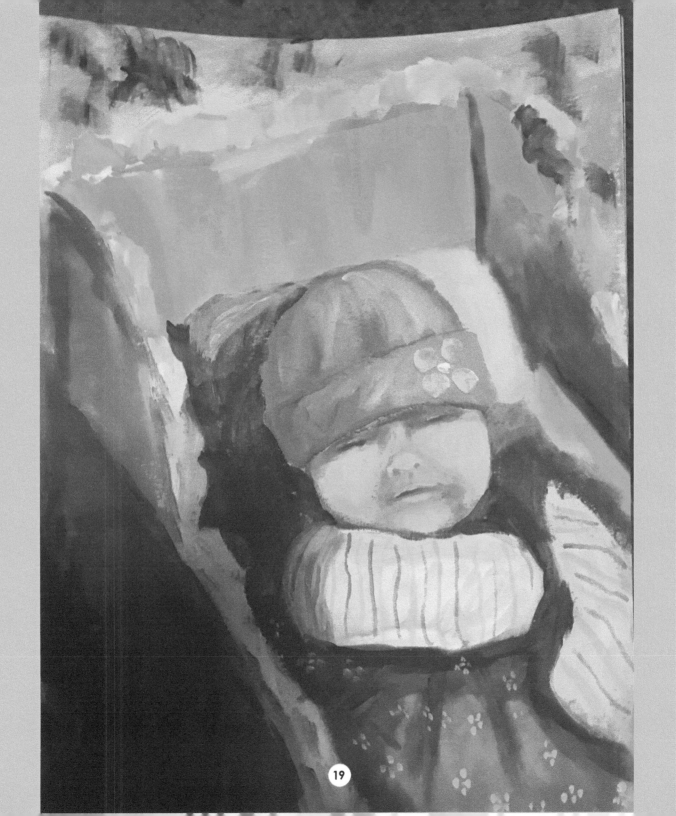

I know you probably think my life is all fun and games, laughter and joy. But it isn't. Everyone has moments that they don't like and I'm no different. There are times at night when I get scared. It is dark and not as noisy as in the daytime. I feel so all alone. I start to cry.

Then there are those times when I don't feel good. My belly hurts and I can't eat or sleep or even play. All I can do is lay there and cry. That is upsetting to those around me. I see the concern on their faces. They pick me up. They hold me and sing to me. They rock me and kiss me Their love pours out over me! Just knowing that they are there, regardless of what they look like in the wee hours of the morning or late at night, fills me with happiness. Seeing them give up their sleep to take care of me shows how much they care about me and love me!

You see, everyone needs someone. I need those that are in my life as much as they need me. Our lives would be so much different if we didn't have each other. But I am glad that we are together and would not want it any other way! Because the way they make me feel is a feeling I would never want to have changed at all. I love my family and friends so very much and would not be the same Person if not for them.

Being held is one of the most joyous things about being small. And since I am very little yet, they carry me around a lot. It is a wonderful sensation to feel their heartbeat against me. Without the feel of their heartbeat I would feel so alone. To me, the heartbeat means love. I love to be loved! It does not matter why they hold me. Just to be in the arms of someone that cares about me helps me to feel safe, secure and of course, loved. That is an experience that everyone should be able to know and enjoy.

To be cared for and cared about is the true meaning of being alive. I want so much to share my happiness and joy with those around me. I cannot wait to tell them how much I care for them and love them. But for now theyhave to see what it means to me by the way I act. They can't help but see the happiness on my face and in the actions I make. Look out for when I can talk though, because I will have a lot to say!

Another reason that I can't wait to get a little older is for the food. I want to be able to choose what I eat. I see my brother and parents eating stuff that smells so good and looks so yummy that I would like to try it, but I need teeth! For now, I am stuck with food that looks nothing like what they all are enjoying. It's not bad stuff now mind you, just different.

They seem to find it amusing when I eat. Some of the stuff tastes weird and I try to get it out of my mouth. Other times it tastes so good I don't want to stop. But whatever my reaction is, they find it funny, and that makes me laugh. Maybe sometime I will share the awful tasting stuff with them. I mean really, why should I eat it if they won't? But the good stuff is all mine!

By now, you can see my life is pretty nice. I have a great family, wonderful friends and lots of good food and fun toys. There may be times when things are not as nice as other times, but that is the way things go. And like I said before: I would not change anything at all.

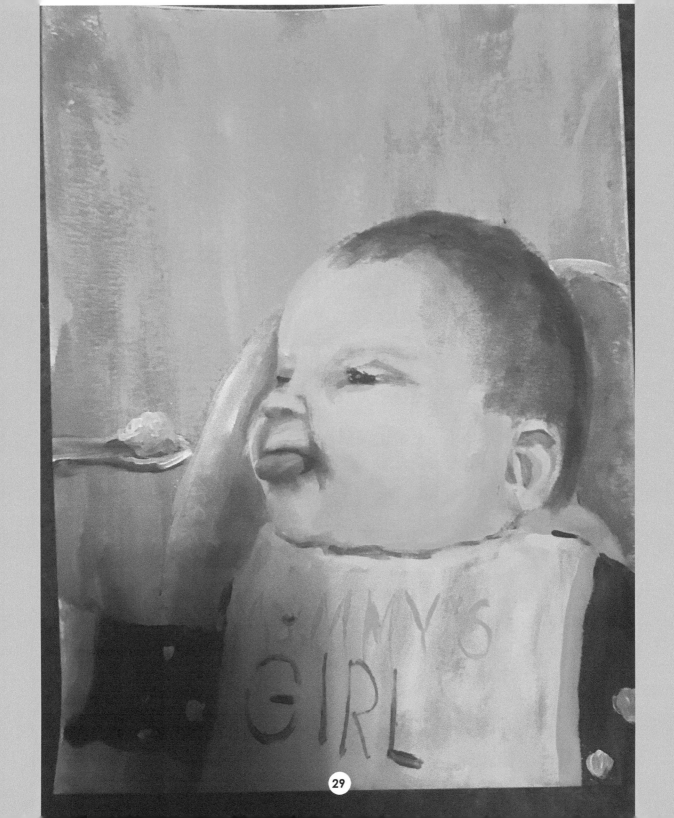

Being happy boils down to several things; love from those around you, feeling safe at all times, a full belly, knowing that you are not alone when sick or scared and of course, a dry diaper!

Every person has a reason to smile. That reason is because that no matter who you are or where you are, you are loved by someone somewhere. Never forget that you have people in your life that love and cherish you for who you are. People that will always care about how you are doing and will be there for you no matter what life brings your way. To those In my life I have something to say;
I LOVE YOU!

Lightning Source UK Ltd.
Milton Keynes UK
UKHW021126181220
375282UK00002B/45